Changing and Growing

Written by Jo Windsor

Rigby

MW00895718

In this book you will see animals changing and growing...

tadpole

caterpillar

bird

Look at this frog.

Look at the eggs.

They are frogs' eggs.

These animals lay eggs.

 Yes? No?   Yes? No?

 Yes? No?   Yes? No?

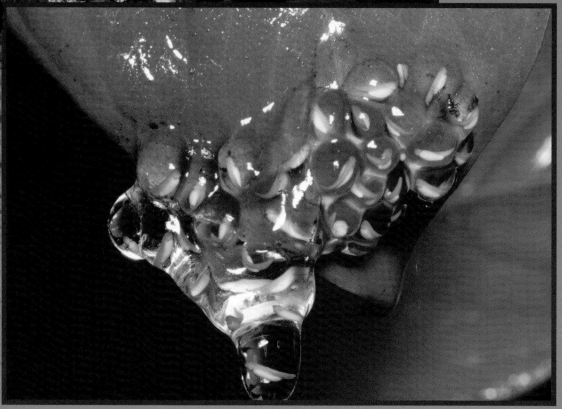

This tadpole has come out of an egg.

It has a big tail.
The tail helps it swim.

Look at the tadpole now!

It has four legs.

It looks like a little frog.

Look at the grasshopper.

It is on a leaf.

Look at the eggs.
The eggs are in the ground.

The eggs will be...

frogs Yes? No?

grasshoppers Yes? No?

birds Yes? No?

The eggs stay in the ground for a long time.

Baby grasshoppers come out of the eggs.

The baby grasshoppers get bigger and bigger.

Then they come out of their skins.

They have a new skin.

Look at the bird.

The bird is on the nest.

The bird has eggs in the nest.
She sits on the eggs.
She keeps the eggs warm.

The eggs will hatch Yes? No?

Baby birds will come out Yes? No?

The baby birds come out of the eggs. They do not have feathers.

Mother bird and father bird feed the babies.

The baby birds get bigger.

Look at the butterfly.
The butterfly is on the leaf.

Look at the eggs.
The eggs are on the leaf.
The butterfly laid the eggs
on the leaf.

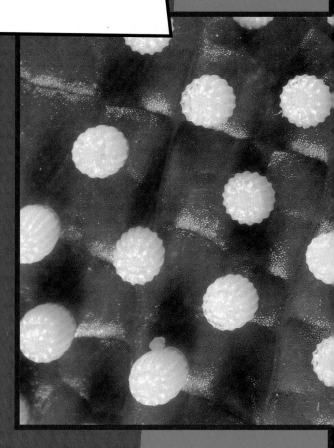

A caterpillar comes out of the egg.
The caterpillar eats and eats.

The caterpillar is in the cocoon.

In the cocoon is...

a caterpillar Yes? No?

a butterfly Yes? No?

a grasshopper Yes? No?

cocoon

The butterfly is coming out.

Look at the butterfly's wings!

Index

Life Cycles

Look at the life cycle of the frog.
Make a life cycle for a butterfly.

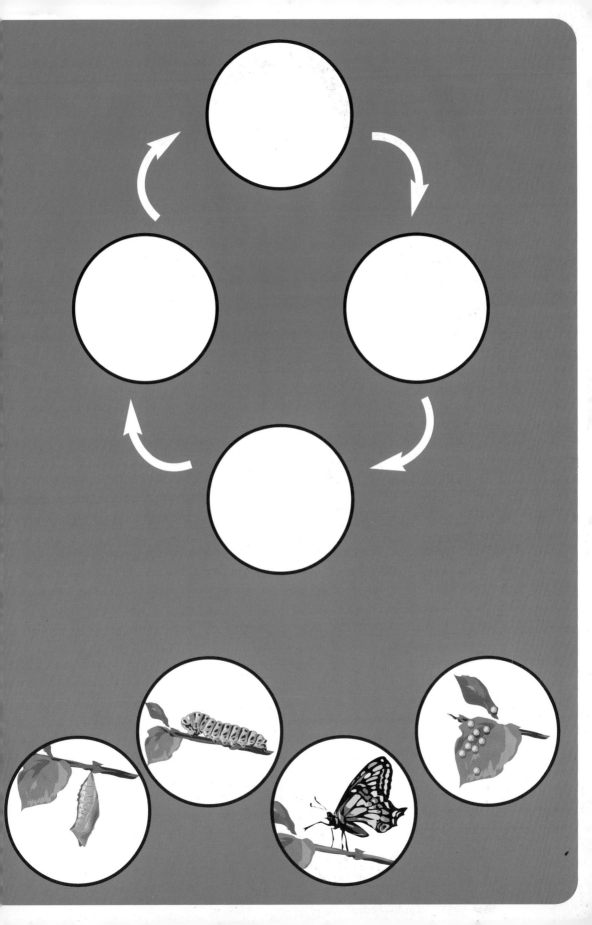

Word Bank

eggs

ground

feathers

leaf

grass

nest